# The Mechanical Copula

*ternberg*Press

# The Mechanical Copula

Sternberg Press

| | |
|---|---|
| The Hare's Course | 9 |
| Penalty for Perfidy | 19 |
| archetypes have no place here | 23 |
| Oestrus | 25 |
| The Island of Scientists | 27 |
| Sixteen Element Course on Mechanical Inelasticity | 33 |
| How You Lost the Stars | 37 |
| 1982, DOOM KNOTS | 41 |
| Death Park | 45 |
| Our Aiguille | 49 |
| Feast of Fear | 51 |
| Mizzle | 53 |
| The Buttered Slice | 57 |
| The Personal Game | 59 |
| Window Strikes | 63 |
| But the past is disappearing, said the pioneer | 75 |
| Spume | 79 |
| The Mechanical Copula | 85 |
| Burger King Drinking | 89 |
| This Heaven | 91 |

# T
# Har
# Cou

What woke Jackie up was the sound of lumpy spillage, urgent on the hall's cork floor. Mark had reached the bathroom before he puked up for a second time, but once again he didn't make it to the toilet. His vomit splashed off the tiles and up against the cistern onto the side of the bath, depositing pale sticky chunks on the red bath mat hanging over its side. Jackie steered him to the toilet bowl where Mark retched to order. Very little came out, he'd already emptied most of it over the floor. She told him to rinse his mouth out, brought him back to bed, and put the washing-up basin and a small cup of water beside him. Then she went back to clean the mess up.

Five hours earlier, they had eaten a three-course meal at St. John. On the way home, Jackie felt utterly full, her stomach so bulging that its skin was taut and shiny. She could have no more shoved another thing into her mouth than that suckling pig she had seen the waiters serving to a big birthday party in the private dining room: its jaws jammed open with a large Bramley apple, which because of roasting looked more like small brown melon. She was stuffed, bloated but maybe not quite sated.

The meal had been Mark's Christmas present to Jackie. She'd eaten at St. John before—well, three times actually, twice with Mark and once with Paddy. The first time was with Paddy, more than two years ago now. She and Mark ate there only on special occasions, her thirtieth birthday and their engagement. Paddy and her had gone there one Tuesday night on the off chance there'd be a free table, they'd just fancied it, that's all.

Mark had booked the table for eight. He was coming directly from work so they'd arranged to meet in the restaurant's bar at a quarter past seven. As 'Manager of Ground Floor Glass & China Department' in the Conran Shop, Mark informed Jackie that there was plenty of tidying up to be getting on with, after the store had closed. Apparently Christmas shoppers were even more demanding and messier than the usual crowd, so he didn't mind staying on an extra half an hour to sort things out. He had ironed his own shirt in the morning before leaving, which was highly unusual, Jackie did all the ironing. She decided to take it, as she thought Mark had meant it as a conciliatory festive gesture.

Teaching at school had finished last Friday and she'd no prep work to do for the pupils until January, so Jackie had already been off work for almost a week. She furiously scrubbed every surface in the flat, slowly prepared thoughtful evening meals, read reams and reams, occasionally tried to take it easy. Mostly though, Jackie slyly avoided doing any of her own artwork, and in reality, it was this that took up most of her time.

If she spent any time brooding on it, that whole thing could get throbbing, complicated and upsetting in Jackie's head. Instead, she targeted her creative energies outwards, teaching art, Mark, and housekeeping, thereby sidestepping the reality of the sticky situation that she had created for herself over the last couple of years.

Mark had been extremely quiet for the past few days, just as he had been both Christmases they'd spent together. Jackie was sure that this was because he was jealous of the amount of time she had off for holidays. He brought it up again and again, basically anytime they were out with his friends or his family. He thought it was side-splitting to crack on about how Jackie spent her time off, lounging on the sofa, in front of the television, watching *Columbo* or *Richard & Judy*.

Jackie guessed that another reason for Mark's silence was that he always got ill at Christmas, just as soon as he'd finished work.

Rather tartly, she commented on it last year, but Mark had gone really moody when Jackie said what she did, so she didn't dare mention it again, even though she continued to think it. Jackie interpreted Mark's especial passivity then as him preparing her (and maybe also himself) for the inevitable: nausea, loss of appetite, scratchy sore throat, night sweats. Considering they were spending Christmas at her ma's boxy two-bedroom flat, she wasn't quite sure how well that one would work out.

Jackie knew she'd not enjoy eating lunch, she was too excited about what bits of animal she was going to consume later. All she really fancied was beans on toast. She had her lunch with a mug of strong tea at the beech IKEA table in the kitchen, eating quickly, without relish. Quite tasty, maybe a little too sweet, but not as bad as those organic ones she'd bought that time from Fresh & Wild, with cinnamon in them. They were foul, like a beany fondue of some order. Jackie thought it was usually best to keep it simple and stick with the classics, after all there's bound to be a reason why they have achieved cult status.

Draining the last of the tea, she flicked through a Waitrose Christmas recipe booklet that had come free through the letterbox, and wondered if any of the meats featured in the pages' recipes would be on the menu later. Very unlikely, she concluded, all too domestic in flavour, hence the fact that they need to be marinated for hours and served in fancy ways. That was one of the main things Jackie liked most about St. John: no messing about, just great big slabs of animal shown to the pan.

After lunch, she washed up the dishes and wrapped her ma's and her sister's presents, she and Mark were flying to Belfast early on Christmas Eve so she wanted to have everything ready. Jackie hated wrapping presents. Mark loved it. He meticulously folded over each edge of the wrapping paper and rolled the tape into tight, flat double-sided loops, so that it couldn't be seen on the outside of the wrap. Next, he tied ribbon tightly around the present and curled lengths of it into spirals with the inside blade of a pair of scissors. Jackie was more concerned about what the present actually was rather than how it had been wrapped. She thought that Mark's particular interest in gift wrapping came from his job at the Conran Shop, always dealing with the sort of people who care more about what's on the outside than on the inside.

Jackie then ironed clothes for the few days she and Mark would be away, she didn't pack them though thinking they'd just get wrinkled. She hung them from the wardrobe door. For wearing to dinner she pressed a black satin swing skirt that tied at the side, and a silk floral bell-sleeved top that tied at the front. Jackie liked getting dressed up to go out; actually both she and Mark did. When he was getting on her nerves, as he had been over the past three days, Jackie made a strenuous effort to focus on the comparatively small, but nevertheless vital number of things that they did still share and enjoy doing together. Dressing smartly, eating well (particularly in swanky restaurants when they could afford it), rearranging the furniture in the flat, watching DVDs of comedy programmes.

It helped her to retain the memory of how irresistible Mark had seemed to her when they first met, that time in the Conran Shop. Spotless, well brought up, and polite, with an impeccably English dry sense of humour. And he had given her a ten percent discount off a Rosenthal china mug she had bought to cheer herself up after Paddy left.

Hard now to believe just how impressed she'd been by Mark's mother and father, who remembered all his friends' and work colleagues' names, and who ate their dinner at a lovely big old scrubbed wooden table in the kitchen! They had, in turn, been charmed by the novelty of her Northern Irish accent, her tasty and honest cooking, her arty background (even though she hadn't produced a painting in over a year) and her intense desire to nurture their son.

Scanning across Mark's neatly buttoned cotton shirts, Jackie considered what a quare change Mark had been from Paddy. Paddy, a big loud lump of a fella who'd scared his fellow students at art college, and just took up so much space. Really, Paddy was just like her. Well, like how she used to be before. Poor stock cautiously sniffing their way out. 'Interchangeable' was how their friends described the two of them, especially when they were drunk.

After college, when they moved to London together, Paddy started to quiet down, maybe even shrink. He certainly seemed considerably smaller in London than he had done in Belfast. Jackie, on the other hand, grew. She stood up straighter, ate as much good cheap food from the Turkish shops in Dalston as she wanted, loved not having to talk to anybody on public transport, and was, in general, greatly relieved to be out of her own culture.

Jackie suddenly realised that she hadn't made the effort to see even one of those old friends since she and Paddy had split up. He went back to Belfast quite quickly after their relationship had cracked, and Jackie, well, Jackie really wanted to stay.

She eased off the engagement ring Mark had bought her, gave it a brisk buff with the tail of her shirt, and pushed it back down on her ring finger. Peasant hands, Mark had joked sweetly when they had to get the jeweller to stretch the ring that Jackie finally settled on, so that it would fit over her knuckle.

When she was growing up, Jackie's family had never once eaten out at a restaurant. She had seen people doing it in programmes and films on television, and thought how *glamorous* it would be to sit at a table, wearing smart clothes, chewing your food carefully, talking and laughing all at the same time.

Once when Jackie was thirteen she dreamt she was an adult having dinner at the Skandia in Belfast—the only restaurant she had ever actually seen—and ordered the Beaver Steak. In the morning, when Jackie told her big sister about the dream, Angela howled so much that she could barely breathe and actually started crying. Jackie got hot and embarrassed because she didn't understand why Angela was laughing.

While she'd been ironing, Jackie listened to her Bing Crosby Christmas CD. She played it when she was alone because Mark wouldn't listen to it, just like he wouldn't listen to her Prince, Edith Piaf, Dean Martin or the Pet Shop Boys CDs. Mark had informed her, fairly early on after they had moved in together, that he only wanted to listen to his music in his flat. He had tried to say it like it was a joke but Jackie didn't find it very funny. She reasoned that Mark was talking shite because technically it wasn't his flat anyway, his parents had bought it as an investment, and both her and him shared the bills.

Jackie was bored, very bored after she had finished ironing, and it was still only four o'clock. She needed to leave the flat at half past six to get to the restaurant for a quarter past seven, so she'd start getting ready at six. Two hours. Knowing that she shouldn't, that it'd spoil the surprise, Jackie did it anyway. She couldn't concentrate on anything else but the prospect of chewing meat. She had bookmarked the St. John website on their computer and looked at it at least once a week to see what was on offer. She looked up the supper menu reassuring herself that Mark wouldn't find out, she always ordered food much more quickly than him. The only thing that might scupper her supper plans was if there was a special on that sounded really tasty. However, Jackie almost always preferred to order from the menu. She had found that when she ordered a special, it was served too quickly, like a sale item that had to be snapped up.

Thursday, 21st December 2006 Dinner Menu. Starters: Native Oysters, £2.00 each. But they only cost 50p each on the dock at Whitstable. I know it's different having them in a restaurant, but that markup would stick in my craw, so I'll not have them, even though I'd quite like to. I'm going to have Smoked Sprats & Pickled Red Cabbage instead, bit festive and I like having fish for starters. £6.10 for the Sprats, I could have had three oysters for that, but then Mark would have eaten one of them and I would have to share some of his starter and it might be something I don't like the look of. The only other thing that I like the look of is the Black Cuttlefish & Onions. I had that before at St. John, not that that would stop me having it again. A shiny satanic non-fishy dish it was, slipped softly down the back of my throat, most pleasurable. For while afterwards, I pretended that the Cuttlefish had dyed the tip my uvula black. Mark said not to be so stupid, that it was just the shadow inside my mouth making it look dark, and that it had most probably always been that colour but I'd never noticed it before. He has a habit of saying things like that when I make a joke and he doesn't get it. Drains the life out of it.

Mains: Goose, Butterbeans & Foie Gras, £19.20. That's very cheap to have foie gras in it, you mustn't get very much. Goose on goose action. Woodcock, wooden cock, £29. Lamb's Tongue, Turnips & Mustard, £14.80. That's making me wonder how many tongues you get per plate, what size they are and whether they are sliced or left whole. I had a nibble of ox tongue once. Mark ordered it when we had lunch with his parents in Bath. Roughly cut into thick square slabs, looked like salt beef, but on closer inspection I could see the taste buds still attached. The meat tasting itself. Hare Saddle & Beetroot, £16.40. That's it, that's what I'm having.

Hare is one of the finest things I have ever eaten. It's in my personal list of the best food, joint first with the sea-salty clam soup I ate beside the ocean with Paddy five years ago, on a cheapy package deal to Lanzarote.

I had the Hare with Paddy as well. We both ordered it, which we thought was boring but we wanted it so much. The big lump of meat sat like a right royal crown rather than a saddle on the plate. It smelt like it was off, a high sweet steam rising from it: almost but not quite foul, like it had been left to hang for too long in a damp poacher's shed, beside the gun that had shot it. Of course, I knew it was perfectly *ripe* and that the meat hadn't been forgotten in a poky shack, more likely it had been matured in a hermetically sealed, hygienic stainless steel cabinet somewhere. But you know, I liked thinking about the meat that way. It titillated me. Paddy concurred, saying the poacher had killed a score of hare that day and at least eight brace of pheasant (actually he said peasants, to which I replied that if they were on the menu, I'd certainly order them, provided that their muddy boots had first been removed).

The Hare was a dense Rothko red, maybe maroon: certainly massier than mauve. Decaying but freshly cauterised on a searing hot griddle, the flesh was the same colour the whole way through, it had needed so little cooking because it had been hung for so long. When I put a lump into my mouth I hardly even needed to chew, the enzymes had done most of that for me already. The meat rested gently on my tongue, dead, just about to become alive again. I bit down on it twice. Paddy and I were masticating together, and I remember thinking how close I felt to him—dreamy and aroused as we both had this meat in our mouths—and that it would pass down the back of our throats, through our gullets, into our stomach, and there be reduced to a mush by all that acid. Slowly moving through our small and large intestines, taking two days to turn into faeces. I hoped that we would both shit out the remains of the Hare at about the same time. It soothed and excited me to think our bodies could be so closely linked, in a way other than sex. On the Thursday morning, two days after me and Paddy had eaten at St. John, I went in to use the bathroom after him. I could smell hare, not shit but sweet hare, as if Paddy had preserved it in his body and it had passed out of him intact.

The smell of Mark's vomit almost made *me* retch as I was scooping it up with handfuls of toilet roll. Runny yet lumpy, the irregular pools that he'd boked across the hall and bathroom floors, were held loosely together by fibrous matter that looked but didn't smell like lightly chewed bananas. The strange thing was that there was no trace of what Mark had eaten earlier. Venison Heart & Pickled Damsons, followed by Rare Roast Beef on Dripping Toast with Beet Greens, then Eccles Cake & Lancashire Cheese. I saw him eating it, but somehow his stomach and intestines had rendered the three courses into a curdled albino mass.

It took ages to clean up, the vomit was so nondescript that I couldn't see properly where it had splashed onto the white bathroom suite, thick clumps of it soaking into the bath mat. I remember thinking the mat would need washing at ninety degrees to get the awful smell out, and that the colour would almost certainly run and then it would be drained, pinkish and spoilt.

pen
f
perfi

This is the story of a bored boy who thought it would be a good idea to simulate a bank robbery.

Conveniently, he was already in possession of a replica revolver that he could bring along with him. The boy also owned a real gun, but remembering the whole point of the holdup was that is was fake, decided it would be a better idea to leave that particular weapon at home. Boredom and pursuit of stimulation afforded the boy the luxury of this sort of spontaneous decision-making: a benefit of which he was normally bereft.

The boy boarded a bus heading into the town centre and alighted at the third bank he saw on the High Street. He ignored two building societies as they didn't quite fit into the concept of a bank robbery, however simulated.

Whilst crossing the street towards his target, the boy formed the demand for the money in his throat. He may even have been lightly mouthing it, except no one was watching him to notice whether he was or not.

The boy entered the bank, which was not too empty and not too full, and proceeded to pretend to hold it up. Knowing as much about bank security as we do (from programmes and films he had watched on television), he pointed the replica revolver at the cashiers, told them to stand away from the counters, and asked the bank manager to collect all the bills from the tills.

Now at this point in the story—just as the cash was being drawn together—the boy experienced a surge of surprise, everyone really seemed to believe his heist, for they were all participating in it. He smirked at the thought, when, at just the very same moment, a heavy bank customer really collapsed, really rattled his last breath, and really died of a heart attack. The boy was incredulous at first, if somewhat perturbed by the blue lips. The other bank customers screamed at the sight and then fell collectively silent.

This diversion gave the bank manager an opportunity to press the silent alarm button under the counter whilst seeming to be packing the last roll of notes. He was glad it wasn't his heart that had given way and gladder still he had made a positive effort to ensure the capture of this menace to society.

The boy could not believe the bank manager was actually handing him the bags of bills over the counter. He decided to take them and leave, so as not to disappoint the bank employees and customers, and exited swiftly through the double glass doors. Everyone was relieved the boy was finally leaving and that it was someone else who had had a heart attack and not them.

The boy looked down at his suede shoes in the sunshine. He wondered where he would get change to pay for a bus ticket home, or if instead he should walk back, when he looks up to see a real policeman, who really shoots on sight, and does.

archety
hav
place h

One persistently fiddles with the top button of her blouse, a little distressed perhaps, whilst another observes her with care and winks towards someone I can't quite see. A single-heeled, black suede shoe droops dejectedly from the hand of its owner, not needed for the nonce. A polished silver pocket watch links a couple together briefly before resting from its chain. Two middle fingers touch slyly for a moment. An index finger breaks a circle to explore an open mouth. Too many hands touch too many faces for me to remember each one. Tired wrists are rubbed, squeezed, or simply inspected. The right knee eases its way out of the thick grey tights, already too late to mend. Many white tissues are consumed, some with tears, most not. Two of the younger women sit on the edge of the kerb, gilding the gutter. What? What are they saying?

Oest

Shoot instead of type.
Slash instead of rewind.
Smother instead of pause.

# Th
# Isla
# Scien

*Nearly a year passed before he perceived that his love was bringing about a change in the vegetation of the pink coomb. He had taken no notice at first of the disappearance of grasses and small seedlings from the places where his own seed was sown. But his attention was caught by the growth of a new plant that he had seen nowhere else on the island. The plant had large, lace-edged leaves which grew in clusters at the level of the earth on a very short stalk. It bore white, sharp-scented blossoms with pointed petals and brown, ample berries which largely overflowed their calyxes. Robinson observed them with curiosity, but thought no more about them until the day when it became unmistakably apparent that they appeared within a few weeks at the precise place where he has sown his seed.*

And everything led to these concentric circles——alternate land and water with the central island flattened and trimmed into a large plain. A long oblong of impossibly perfect proportions, unthinkable in scale, unbelievable in fecundity, yielding to even the most barren of imaginations.——————The circles were enclosed by a sea wall, constructed from stacks of flat stone slabs, which rather than seeming forbidding felt alive and built-up with terraces of houses and municipal buildings.—————The continent was blessed with plentiful mineral resources, timber—a wide variety of fauna, flora, wild vegetation, and vernal fruit trees. The intriguing thing is that the population did not simply consume these gifts of the gods, but rather chose to undertake massive building projects: for example, linking the rings of land with wooden bridges and digging a canal————————three hundred feet wide————one hundred feet deep————which resembled a harbour with a mouth broad enough to welcome even the largest of vessels.

————Even though it represented the gateway to an island, the port did not feel isolated, but was instead crowded with swarms of international merchant ships, from which rose an incessant din of yelling, bawling and shanty singing throughout the day and night.

————————The ziggurats, palaces and shrines were extremely rich and ornate, even somewhat gauche in appearance.————A symptom of affluence and confluence rather than influence.————

*That which is to receive all forms should have no form; as in making perfumes they first contrive that the liquid substance which is to receive the scent shall be as inodorous as possible; or as those who wish to impress figures on soft substances do not allow any previous impression to remain, but begin by making the surface as even and smooth as possible.*

What they had to think about was how to spend their time and how to tell everybody about what they had done. This bifurcated vacation was obviously a story in two parts.————They were creating at the limits rather than in the middle of the community and————surely a good thing————since the main problem with this type of activity tends to occur when one tries to decide in which way tribes change when engaged in extensive contact with each other————————and in which ways they do not.

————————The rubric there was smudged. This first contact————the blush————————the lack of functional interrelations, could I am told————————last for just one day or for the whole week————————————depending on the particular family units.————It

took a while to recognise the concept of total social fact was
less static than they had been led to believe, than we all had been
led to believe.

*To them I have incurred a debt which I can never repay, even if, in
the place in which you have put me, I were able to give some
proof of the tenderness which they inspire in me and of the gratitude
which I feel towards them by continuing to be as I was among
them, and as, among you, I would hope never to cease from being:
their pupil, their witness.*

Cultivated from a multitude of distinct yet connected planes, each
irrigating the entire field and its entire range of activity——this
general inventory, when understood together, came to constitute
a society. In time, most were glad of the local knowledge and
proactively engaged with the native customs and sports. The search
for causes ends with the assimilation of an experience that is at
once internal and external.

*We have consultations, which of the inventions and experiences
which we have discovered shall be published, and which not; and
take an oath of secrecy for the concealing of those which we
think fit to keep secret, though some of those which we do reveal
sometimes to the state, and some not.*

Objectively remote, subjectively concrete————————the
particular strain of inductive science enacted during that time
proved very fruitful to the participants. There could be no doubt
their visit had informed them in a variety of ways: new sights, new
games, new catches, new ideas, new ways of working. In time, mark
making and human gesture transformed their shared experience,
causing a structural modification to take place.——————Their

new skills and perceptions gradually pooled together to become a meaningful whole.———This tracking could be seen to express or rather compress time. The sifting————measuring and exhibiting of individual sensations———in a space far away from the island——————————————————————never changing in scale or temperature consolidated the contributors————and ————whilst they were never all in the same place at the same time, they had become a group.

# Sixte
# El
# Cour
# Mech
# Inelas

n
ement
se on
anical
icity

(After Henri Bergson)

 1 Two
 2 Men
 3 Are
 4 Eating
 5 A
 6 Clown.
 7 One
 8 Asks
 9 The
10 Other,
11 Does
12 This
13 Taste
14 Funny
15 To
16 You?

# How Y
## lo
## the St

Apparently you have abnormally large optic nerves. Whilst this is not necessarily an immediate cause for concern, the ophthalmologist tells you it might be an early indicator of glaucoma; just to be sure, he wants to test the range of your peripheral vision. He leads you out of his consultancy room and into the hallway, where there's an adult-sized ovoid machine positioned awkwardly in the corner.

The ophthalmologist instructs you to place the black plastic eye patch over your left eye, and to position your chin onto the black plastic rest. As far as you can make out, both appear to be made from the same stuff. You wonder if they were manufactured from the same material, in the same place, at approximately the same time. Your chin fits surprisingly snugly onto the black plastic rest, you feel assured by this, as evidence of the average nature of your facial features. After all, you can't help but feel more than a little worried about having larger than normal optic nerves.

Placing a cold cubiform controller in your right hand, the ophthalmologist pushes your finger down on a button using the pressure of his hand above yours. You wonder why he didn't demonstrate this before you were told to place your head in the machine.

The first thing you notice is nothing. It takes your eyes a little while to get used to this (a novel sensation); after ten seconds, you can't remember looking at anything else. Directly in front of you is a miniscule red glowing dot, just below it, aligned in a short row, three marginally bigger black pocks in the moulded plastic.

It takes you a few seconds to figure out these holes are actually bored into the fabric of the machine, and not just tiny perfect circles rendered lightly on its surface.

Dim grey lights begin to appear in an irregular sequence all around the inside of the dome. Each time you feel confident you've definitely seen one, however faint, the ophthalmologist instructs you to press the controller's button: It registers your selection with what sounds like (but surely can't be, can it?) a brief sigh. The lights grow more indistinct and less regular. You were told you've got to keep your head in this machine for four minutes per eye. You're already getting tired.

You think to yourself: What am I looking for?

The back bedroom. Small. Small but big enough for two people to sleep in comfortably, although it was never comfortable. Planted along the right-hand wall, a chest of drawers which had been in the house for as long as you could remember.

Put together from thin cheap wood, the drawers were surprising light. Each time you pulled them out, you registered the same slight jolt of disbelief that something so flimsy could actually hold anything. They squealed and squeaked, an uneven cry that didn't diminish with use. Squeal out. Squeak in. Very resistant. Very resentful.

Badly made? Yes, certainly. Cheap like all the other furniture in the house, and indeed the house itself. Complaining. Groaning. Unhappy. Trapped.

Pause.

A low chutter, the ovoid machine relaxes into a breather. The ophthalmologist tells you to take the black plastic eye patch off your left eye, and to put it over your right eye instead. Wheeze. Begin again.

When the drawers were eased out, it wasn't possible to see the original inside colour of their wood at all. The outside surface was coated with decades' worth of paint; when viewed side on, the cracked corner of one of the drawers reads as the rings in a tree trunk.

Layers of shades from the same palette but no less distinguishable for that. Overwhelmingly yellowing at the bottom, redolent of tired gloss that can't be bothered to promote a shiny surface. Varying hues from there on up: very yellow, yellow, less yellow, slightly yellow, a smidgen of yellow, magnolia, cream, ivory, a hint of white, slightly white—never quite achieving brilliance even when freshly coated. The thin wood drank in the paint's brightness, tainting it, reminding the outside layers how unhappy the inside really was.

Sick, like.

Your peripheral vision is average. Not brilliant, not amazing, not supranormal, but not bad. The point of your chin hurts, and your eyelid is clammy when you peel off the black plastic eye patch.

The things you've seen. It'll be at least eighteen months until you see them again.

# 1982,
## 00
## Kno

I walk everywhere. Walking is of course free, and as we are very poor this is a primary consideration. I am too young to work, there's nothing to do at home, walking fills my time.

At the weekends, I walk with him. We always follow the same route, the same sequence of places. I like that. We talk as we walk. I like that too.

I begin to sort through the contents of bins on my journey. I can't recall the exact location where I started, but think it was probably outside the back of the courthouse. What I am sure about is I'm always alone when I do it.

At first, I chose only bins sited somewhere secluded, so I couldn't be observed. Now when I feel compelled to look through each one I pass. I don't care where they are or who sees me. I empty each bin's contents onto the pavement, spread it out and inspect it carefully.

Whilst shifting through the piles of rubbish, I read the wrappings, the junk mail, the newspapers, the packaging, the shopping lists, the letters and the magazines.

Gradually, I witness the mass accumulation of brainpower expended in their production.

All of this printed matter is familiar. I understand the discarded instructions for electrical appliances even though I have no use for them, the newspapers are sometimes old, often new. The letters are always addressed to people who I don't know personally, but recognise just the same.

A thousand voices speak to *me* directly.

I alone listen. No one else wants to hear. That's why I must look through every bin so as not to show any favouritism.

I observe most people are revolted by my daily habit. It seems they are disgusted with the notion that such unwanted matter may still be read, may still hold meaning.

This activity becomes indispensable to me. I leave my house early in the morning and come back late at night. I never take any of it home. It takes such a long time to work my way through so much stuff.

Over time, as the world's words leak into me, I begin to leak out.

I don't walk with him at the weekends anymore. I don't talk to him or listen to him. I'm far too busy with my bins.

Dea
p

Then just as I go through the big gates at the side of the park, I spy a white plastic patio chair facing a particularly top-heavy oak tree. On closer inspection, the chair appears to have been carefully positioned so that its sitter is exactly facing the tree trunk at eye level.

I'm experiencing a strong desire to sit down on the chair, to take in the trunk in detail; the comprehensive glory of its picture plane, scenic cracked bark, and parched lichen blooms: its general arborescence. But this side of the park is ever so busy, and, to be honest, I'll probably get very embarrassed if anyone actually sees me studying a tree.

I continue my circuit of the park. There, by the overflowing litterbin, a mature *turdus merula* with a Twix wrapper clamped tightly in its beacon-bright orange beak; the gold and red of the wrapper, together with the colour of the bird's beak, suit each other well. I wonder if the bird has actually eaten the Twix, or just likes the look of the wrapper. I'd like to see the nest that that wrapper becomes woven into: shiny.

I prefer my nature with a bit of plastic in it: well defined, open at 7.00am, closed at 6.30pm. Then I know exactly where I am. Otherwise I don't understand, nature pushes me out, keeping me at a blade's length. The countryside scares me shitless. Lost, almost, but not quite alone, in damp silence, save for legions of little animals that can see you in the dark, circling, with rows of sharp teeth and claws.

A screech. I turn quickly to witness a glossy *corvus corone* tumbling, the bird falling beak-first from the tree into long grass below. An exaggerated scuffle. A black, feathered clump splayed out flat on its back; now extending its wings like a broken umbrella, trying to right itself through a one-hundred-and-eighty-degree rotation. When the bird eventually manages to stand up, it looks very confused and just stands there stock-still, blinking for some minutes. Can it remember how it got from the tree's branches to the ground? Was it pushed, or did it forget how to fly?

Twenty-three years ago, walking along May Street, Mother suddenly and without warning starts thwacking me hard on the crown of my head with a rolled-up newspaper she's unsheathed from her shopping bag. She's spotted a *vespula vulgaris* crawling into my hair and is trying to kill it. No! Mother might well squash the angry little insect, sting and all, right into my scalp.

I hear my steps, hollow, as I cross the wooden bridge spanning the park's stream to exit. Lately, the weather here has been very muggy, humid, and cloudy; the pungent algae which cloak this stream love close weather, rapidly coating the water, reeking from edge to edge.

A tiny *anas platyrhynchos* is emitting the most distressing squealing sound; very loud for something so small, very human for something so obviously not.

I've always wondered why the stench from the algae was so bad, now I think I know: There is a cache of dead baby birds suspended below, gradually decaying, waiting.

I'm staring, it's so hard to see what is going on exactly. What I can make out is that the algae are stuck to the baby bird's back and wings, weighing it down, pulling it too far down into the stream. Look, the tiny bird's mother is pecking at her baby's back, trying to remove each speck of alga one by one, but she's not helping at all. Rather, with each peck, the smaller bird is sinking further down into the water. The algae seem to be thickening the water, making not only the surface but also the depth below slop around thick and soupy.

The last thing I see is the baby bird going down into the stream and not coming up again.

And now I'm thinking about that incident in Kensington Gardens twelve years ago, when a man murdered his lover and dumped her body into the Italian Gardens' ornamental lake. She floated under giant lily pads for three weeks, undiscovered, until a *larus minutus* took something from her face, later dropping one flaccid eye near an ice-cream van.

0.
a.

Mama started it. Piero pushed it. Sophia dodged it. Papa stayed out of it. And Annunciata, well, Annunciata always finished it.

fea
of

"That one time I was over in London, me and the brother-in-law, fair few jars in us, goes till Soho with a torch. Aye, a Saturday night it was. Not till the dirty shaps, mind you, we went till that fuckin wop street… What d'ye call it? Black begs filled up with all the leftover wop food… Stinkin! Stinkin so it was! Down a back entry, there was this big black fuck-off rat, froze in the light of the torch so it did. The brother-in-law'd brought his airgun with him, so I takes a potshot at the cunt. Holy shit! Must've clipped the back of the body, it was screaming like a wee baby. There was millions of them rats everywhere, fat fuckers eating all that wop food. Right enough, I used to like wop food meself. No fuckin way I'd ever touch it now."

m

The taxi window to my right won't close properly. Cocked open a quarter of an inch, letting in a determined spray of light rain, which, while the cab is in motion, lands right on my lap, making its way through the denim of my jeans and onto the skin on my legs.

A familiar feeling. Not entirely unpleasant.

Belfast has this way of raining that's peculiarly Northern Irish. I've never been soaked anywhere else the way I've been soaked here. It's subtle. It's persistent. It's drenching. A steady, penetrating mizzle that works its way down to your knickers and then keeps on going, leaving you with the feeling even your heart has been wet right through. That's the way it's raining now.

People and cars have learnt to deal with this relentless patter. They have short lives. They decay rapidly. They expire before their time. Both, however, have developed long memories to compensate, tracking their way back and forth across a saturated city that's really too small to be a city at all. More of a brusque town that got too big for its boots in the seventies, left today with the feeling it can't live up to its past.

This taxi and its driver are no exception. They both welcome the rain, love it even. The driver keeps the windscreen wipers going at too slow a speed to deal efficiently with the steady flow, to the point where I'm wondering whether he can see out in front of him properly at all.

The cab approves, whinnying and shivering at the traffic lights, its lethargic wipers responding to each shimmering sheet of mizzle with a halfhearted admonish.

*Shhh-shhh. Shhh-shhh. Shhh-shhh. Shhh-shhh.*

# T
# Butter
# S

Everyone in the street knew Mr Forte's son interfered with the loaves of bread on sale in their shop.

An outsized thirteen year old, the boy had surprisingly long white teeth, blushing brown eyes and an awkward ear. As he was always in the shop, I can't see how he ever went to school; he could count though, and read the shopping lists brought in by children from their mothers, so he must have had an education of some sort.

The first time I heard about what Forte's son was doing was from my mate Martin. He told me that on Tuesday afternoon he'd bought a pan loaf to make corned beef sandwiches for his lunch. Martin said he hadn't realised the bread had been fiddled with until he was halfway through it on Wednesday morning. One slice had been buttered. A thin layer had been spread carefully to the crust. Martin ate it.

Almost every day after that, a neighbour would discover some intervention in their bread purchase. One slice only. Always towards the middle of the loaf. At first, it was only butter but soon a variety of toppings appeared, not necessarily sequential in terms of culinary ambition: crab paste, jam, margarine, Marmite, honey, dripping.

Not one customer complained to Mr Forte. They accepted the altered slice as they supposed it had been offered: in love.

# perso
# ga

he
nal
me

4.37am. Thursday. Silence.

ME: It's dark.

ME: What a piece of work is man!

ME: I sleep for an hour or two at most. Sometimes in short bursts together but more often not. I cannot distinguish my sleep from my thoughts. Have I been asleep? How long have I been asleep?

ME: How noble in reason!

ME: If only there was someone who could hear me and would say yes, or no, the response is of little consequence. That I have been heard is the matter of most importance.

ME: How infinite in faculties!

ME: At that time I dreamt the most precise minds, the finest entrepreneurs were far behind me. My skills had swelled to split the container, which tried in vain to restrain them. That is why I am. That is why I become.

ME: In form and moving, how express and admirable!

ME: I traverse extraordinarily long distances in the lucid moments, characterised by hyperphysical leaps and extramundane bounds. I cover so much ground in a matter of seconds, as to make a mockery of clock time.

ME: In action how like an angel!

ME: Fallen from grace, I exist between hard and soft spaces, where fluid supports me. I float.

ME: In apprehension: how like a god!

ME: And yet, how else could it have begun?

ME: How like a god! How like a god! How like a god!

# Wind
# Str

# wkes

Through my window I can see 3 windows. Each is the window to a kitchen. Each kitchen has a different household living in it. Each household performs approximately the same domestic tasks at the same time. I assume they continue to do these things when I'm not watching, and whilst I can't be absolutely sure about this, the evidence would seem to suggest so.

There's always someone in at least 1 of the kitchens. Even now, as I sit here typing this, I can see the light from Left Window and Middle Window in my peripheral vision. I can make out soft, dark blobs moving around, disrupting the glow. The rest of the rooms in the flats must be built back out behind the kitchens, like living in a corridor!

The best view of the 3 kitchens is from my bedroom, not from this room. The bedroom window is more centrally placed, almost directly opposite the middle kitchen window, but not quite, it's slightly off to the left. That does annoy me, yes, but I try not to dwell on it. I can still get a fair eyeful of all 3 windows simultaneously and that's compensation for the lack of symmetry.

I'm on the fourth floor and so are they, although they are a good bit lower down than me, my floor feels like it's 1 higher than theirs, which of course it's not. Interestingly, the rooms in my flat are about the same height as theirs, so my building must have thicker floors. I like that, nice and solid and secure. Their block is really quite close to mine, we're only separated by a slatted wooden fence and a tarmac driveway that leads to this building's garages. Not that I ever use my garage of course. I don't have a car, I have everything I need delivered to my door.

I've lived here now for 6 months and 6 days. Today is 6$^{th}$ June

2006. This pleases me greatly, in fact, that's why I've started writing this journal today. I don't like just doing things for no specific reason. I'm a very busy man.

I've been thinking about putting down my observations on the facing flats for the last 4 months now. It's taken me just over 2 months to teach myself how to use this PC properly. I read a book to help me learn, *1001 Computer Hints and Tips: A Practical Guide to Making the Most of Your PC and the Internet*, bought it from Amazon, delivered right to my door. I selected that particular book because it's produced by Reader's Digest: that's a brand I can trust. I worked through 10 pages per day, sometimes more if the section had lots of examples or illustrations in it, and not so many hints or tips. It has 352 pages and is hardback. Generally, I prefer hardbacks, they sit flatter on the desk when the pages are open.

I bought this Compaq desktop PC 2 weeks after I moved in and set it up with broadband. I'd read in a free catalogue from PC World that came through my letterbox that broadband is much quicker than conventional dial-up, I like things that are quick and efficient. It didn't take long to install, there was a disk I had to insert into the computer and then all I had to do was keep pressing the *Next* button until the screen said, *Installation Complete*.

\*\*\*

The 3 kitchens opposite are of average size, like oblong boxes really, mine is smaller (11 x 6 feet) although it looks just as big because I don't have a table and chairs or as much kitchenware. Plus my kitchen is a lot tidier than theirs, maybe because I don't spend so much time in it. They spend hours preparing, cooking, and serving food to their families and friends, boiling up huge pots, steaming up their kitchen windows, obscuring my view. I prefer to live alone: always have.

Middle Window spends most of her day, every day except Saturday, in the kitchen. She starts alone at 6.30am, dressed in a white terry-towelling bathrobe, before she gets her 3 children up.
I have never seen her husband, so I've surmised that:
1. He works away all the time. This is very unlikely as I'm sure he would at least get some holidays.
2. He is dead. This would be very tragic considering she is so good-looking, and the children are so little.
3. He has left them. That would be odd, she doesn't look sad.

First thing Middle Window does in the morning is brew real tea in a big shiny Brown Betty teapot, and squirt honey from a plastic bottle (the bottle is shaped like a bear, with a yellow cap that looks like a top hat) onto 1 round of toast. Then she drinks 2 mugs of the tea and eats the toast, sitting alone at the pink Formica-topped table. I was surprised the first time I got a good look at that table in there, it seems so old-fashioned for such a young family. As a boy, I grew up eating meals at a table like that in the early 50s, sitting alone and swinging my bare legs against its chrome-plated legs. I'm into modern furniture now.

I like to have my breakfast standing at the bedroom window watching her. I've got a little plastic tray I use to carry my mug, Brown Betty teapot, tea strainer, and toast in from the kitchen. I bought them all from the Home & Garden section on eBay Express 3 weeks ago. I have a tall imitation-pine bedside table that I move around depending on whether I am sitting up in bed, or standing at the window, so the tray goes on that.

I always hold the plate under the toast while I am eating for 2 main reasons:
1. So the crumbs don't fall over my bathrobe. It's really hard trying to shake them all out of the terry-towelling.
2. So the honey doesn't drip onto the floor. This happened once—it was a complete nightmare sponging it out of the carpet.

I tried using both Carbona Stain Devil #5 Fat, Grease & Oil and Carbona Stain Devil #2 Ketchup & Sauce on it, but I am sure I can still feel a sticky patch if I walk there in my bare feet.

\* \* \*

I just bought a digital camera and another computer book online before I started writing this. The camera is a Kodak EasyShare with an advanced digital zoom. *There are no hassles with it, just beautiful pictures. It's that easy. And that incredible.*

The book is called *Practical Projects for Your PC: How to Make Full Use of Your Computer's Creative Potential*. Like my other computer book, it's published by Reader's Digest, has 352 pages and is hardback. I found *1001 Computer Hints and Tips: A Practical Guide to Making the Most of Your PC and the Internet* very easy to use, so I decided I would stick with the same brand. My plan is to unleash both my own and my computer's creative potential once I have learnt how to do it. This is an exciting challenge for me. I'm going to work up to it by closely following the instructions in the book.

I bought both items from Amazon, it's such a great place to buy a wide variety of products at reduced rates. The book cost me £20.39, that's a saving of 32% off the R.R.P., and because I bought the camera at the same time, the postage is free. Plus I didn't have to leave the flat to buy them, I don't like having to leave here now unless I really have to. I've got such a lot to do.

\* \* \*

I took some pictures of myself today with the digital camera, just to practice. At first it was a bit embarrassing, but the more I took (27 by the end of the first session) the more I enjoyed it. Holding the camera at arm's length, I experimented with and without a flash, and found that no flash was better because it made me look natural.

I need to work out how to use the timer, so that I can take full body shots rather than just my head and shoulders. My plan is to take photographs of myself everyday from lots of different angles. I am not sure how I'll display them in my flat yet, I need to give that some more thought.

\* \* \*

Yesterday, I started taking photographs of the 3 kitchens opposite. Each day, I will download the images I've taken of them, and of myself, from the camera into a folder I've created specially on the desktop of my computer. I know you're not really supposed to keep valuable files on your desktop, but as I'll be working on them regularly I need to have easy access. The folder is called *Who Are You?*

I was inspired to call it this by the fact that The Who's song 'Who Are You?' is the theme tune for *CSI: Crime Scene Investigation*, my favourite programme on television. The original show based in Las Vegas is definitely the finest of the 3 *CSI* series for 2 reasons:

1. Because it focuses most closely on the CSI's actual procedures to solve crimes. The level of detail is so impressive, I am sure it must really be like that.
2. Because Gil Grissom is, by far, the best team leader. He's the only boss who is really interested in the science of it all, the truth. *CSI is not a job for Grissom, it is an expression of who he is as a person, the perfect synthesis of personality and profession.* That's what it says on the *CSI* website. I believe it, because each and every week Grissom demonstrates it through his actions.

\* \* \*

My camera has an advanced digital zoom on it, so the photographs I take with it are really very detailed and therefore very effective. I can see much better into the kitchens with the zoom lens than I could with just my naked eye from the bedroom window. And when I've downloaded the images onto my PC and zoom in even closer, I can even spot lots more I hadn't noticed before: for example, whether the bowl of fruit is full or half empty; if the tea towel is folded over the oven door handle, or hanging from a plastic hook on the side of a wall unit; how full the fridge door is with soft drinks, beer, wine, or milk; and when the big sink tap was last cleaned by how shiny it is.

\*\*\*

Last Tuesday, Middle Window put a set of wooden Venetian blinds up on the window. She came back with them mid-morning, after she had dropped off her 2 girls at school. The little boy sat watching her from his highchair, he had something red in his hand and was chewing on it, but it was too small for me to see properly. He is always so well-behaved, I hardly ever see him crying. She put the blinds up herself—it took her half an hour.

Since then, the blinds have been pulled down all day and all night, tilted to a slant facing the window, completely obscuring my view of what's happening inside the kitchen. How very annoying! What a silly thing to do! That'll mean an awful lot of extra cleaning for her, what with the grease from all that food she brews up for those 3 children sticking to the beech slats. She'll be sorry, and then she'll take them down. Let's hope she realises her mistake sooner rather than later.

\*\*\*

I've been taking photographs of the windows opposite for 6 weeks now. I'm still taking photos of all 3 windows, even though Middle Window nearly always looks the same because of the blinds. The only difference I can tell for sure is whether the light is on or not. I can just about make out how many of them are in there, and where they are in the room, by the shapes that their bodies make in the dull ray of the kitchen light.

I must have all 3 windows, so I am persisting. I find the discrepancy in my evidence very disturbing. I need the pictures of the 3 kitchens to have exactly the same amount of detail.

I've been trying to think of a way to make them all match, but haven't thought of a good enough one yet. Plus I know I'll be proved correct about Middle Window having to take those Venetian blinds down, so it's just a matter of time.

\*\*\*

Something disturbing just happened.

As usual, I was taking my morning quota of photographs out of my bedroom window. It was between breakfast and lunch, 11.42am to be precise, I checked the exact time on my camera. All 3 windows looked busy, making lunch etc., when I think Right Window saw me pointing the camera at her. I have a photograph I took at the moment when she sees me—I've just looked at it big on the computer screen—she's squinting straight into the lens, like she can't see properly what it is. Maybe she couldn't? I pulled back from the window and shut my blinds (I bought approximately the same set as Middle Window, mine are from John Lewis online), usually I keep the slats horizontal so that I can poke the small camera lens through while I look at the image on the small screen at the back of the camera. I don't like Right Window looking at me. I'm investigating them, not the other way round.

I'm sure none of them have ever seen me before, surely I would have noticed them noticing me. I'll wait until early evening before I take some more pictures.

To keep myself busy, I made soup in my new Presto pressure cooker. I'd never cooked in one before. But now, having actually used it I can report it's a very quick, efficient way to cook. I'm hugely busy these days, even more so than before I retired, so the pressure cooker will save me lots of precious time. I'll cook a few days' meals in one go and then store them in the fridge or the freezer. I don't like being away from my window for too long at meal times because, of course, that's when there's most action in the kitchens.

I spent the remainder of the afternoon taking a series of photographs I've been planning for a while now, I had to wait until the Faithful economy tripod stand arrived, which it did yesterday morning. The tripod together with the camera's timer is a much more effective way to take full-length photographs of myself than how I'd been doing it before. This afternoon, I set up the scenarios I wanted to take pictures of first and then stepped into them. There was a lot of detail to get right, in terms of the exact position I stand in and at which angle, so it took quite a long time. The light in my kitchen is perfectly sufficient for the photographs, in fact, it's very lifelike, so I didn't need to use the flash.

\*\*\*

Left Window always cooks her food in a pressure cooker. Each day, she makes either a soup or a stew and then she and her husband eat their way through it. She's too frail to lift the pot off the hob when it's full, so she just ladles the food directly out of the pressure cooker into their bowls or onto their plates. I think that's very unhygienic, especially in warmer weather. They have the same thing for lunch and dinner, except once a week, on Wednesdays, when they have another old person round in the early afternoon: then they eat soft floury rolls filled with ham or cheese.

Right Window's son came for lunch on Sunday. It's only the second time I've ever seen him. He must look like his father. She roasted a small chicken and watched him eat most of it in silence, perched at her wooden breakfast bar. She didn't have anything to eat herself, unusual for her, she always eats a lot when her friends come to visit. After his dessert, her son hung up a net curtain on the kitchen window and then left. Curtains are really disgusting things to have in a kitchen! Not only will they get grey and grubby, they'll stink too! What is she thinking?

\*\*\*

I spotted Right Window in Left Window's kitchen today. I've never seen her there before. The 2 of them sat down at the table opposite the freestanding cooker and talked for almost 1 hour. I don't like that, messy. I wonder where Left Window's husband was?

I didn't want to take any photographs of Right Window in that kitchen, it's wrong for her to be out of her place. I watched them anyway, to see how long she would stay, so that I could resume taking my photographs when she left. After all, Left Window is the only 1 of the 3 kitchens I can still see into properly.

As she got up from the table, I saw Right Window turning round towards my window, I stepped back and sat down on my bed for 2 minutes, and then got back up and stood at the window again. When Right Window had gone, Left Window went out of the kitchen too. She never usually leaves the kitchen at this time, very annoying it was too because I needed to complete the afternoon's quota of photographs.

\*\*\*

Left Window and her husband didn't come back into the kitchen until much later. It was dark so she had to put the light on, that's why I was startled to see there was someone else with them. They never normally have anyone round in the evenings.

Their visitor laid a long roll (about 5½ feet) down on the blue melamine worktop to the right of the cooker beside the window. He cleared the dishes away from the sink area and climbed up onto it with a drill in his left hand. Unusual he should be left-handed.

He drilled on either side above the window and screwed something small I couldn't make out into each of the holes. Then, he hung up a mint-green roller blind. I can't be sure yet if it's made from plastic or fabric.

\*\*\*

It's taking longer than I'd expected to get the hang of cutting and pasting these photographs of myself onto the 3 backgrounds. I'm persisting though, referring to the Reader's Digest book and following the instructions exactly to the letter. You know, I think every day I'm getting a little better.

But th
pas
disapp
said
pio

e
t is
aring,
he
eer

*As I was saying dear heart...*

She continued in the tone of a cone licked by a tense tongue. Not wishing to delay her tale further than it had been already by the twittering aviator she intermittently referred to as her pinion, her bird's eye, but most regularly her quill.

*In a conurbation of this scale, it proved devilishly tricky to find a construction tall enough for my experiment, let alone attempt to gain access and scale it too. Security measures—though not quite so stringent as they had been in even the last five years—were still strictly enforced, and justly so, for who knows what the urban citizenry would do amongst themselves if they were not vigorously invigilated and pinched back tightly into their own mortality... ?*

*It was an inordinately time-consuming task to identify a superstructure of the correct height: a concrete cathexis was what I was really after. I found it eventually, after a four-month rally of daily reconnaissance missions. Only to discover, of course, it had been there all the time...*

*I found the floating to be absolute apodictic ecstasy. And, believe me, after all my meticulous planning, detailed dreaming, drafting and redrafting of routes, I'd been biding my time to experience quite such a rush of rapture. Oh! The pendency! I found that I could navigate my aerial gesticulations quite precisely, but softly-softly-susurrating, suspended in the air vents. Deviant, temperate May Day weather, probably prevailing because of scanty peephole ozone...*

*The gist of this virgin flight was a light but insistent clinch between my thumb and forefinger, therein retaining—in kid gloves so to speak—a feather. When all at once I chanced to remember the traditional assumption, the orthodox abstract, that hominids, such as my fine tellurian self, cannot in actuality fly...*

Hit the ground hard, but stood up immediately to avoid embarrassment.

*I was flying until I remembered I should not be.*

Spu

Jim. Are you asleep, Jim?

You know I've never been a good sleeper. I spend large chunks of my sleeping time awake in pursuit of irrational details, proposed recipes, conceptual vacuuming and general nitpicking. I'm so glad when I lie beside you, you switch off like an electric light bulb. *Phutt:* out like that. I can almost see your eyes beginning to close as your head lowers towards the pillow. Like a little girl's doll you are.

Blessed. Blessed I am to have found you.

For as I struggle, pushing and pulling the pillow up, then down to support my head—or rather support my neck supporting my head—I watch you snoozing soundly, thin eyelids gently undulating, as your eyeballs watch your dreams. That's when I click just how very lucky I am. Lucky you cannot see how much I covet your ability to sleep so well, to have had forty-six years worth of peaceful dreaming, content in your own skin, while I'm crawling out of mine trying to find my own sleep.

I am timid in these murky moments of envy, so I remind myself once more of how fortunate I am. Fortunate you've never been able to stay awake long enough to see how selfish I am when I can't sleep. Grief overtakes me: my shame hugs you, gripping greedily, hoping you'll wake in my arms. You don't. The bed-space around your body is hot, much warmer than at my side of the bed: I grasp you even tighter, hoping to squeeze out some sleep.

Once I nipped your shoulder, hot and hard, spurred on by my fury, my distress at losing you for the night. I wanted to tell you about the lightning quick connections that had begun to take place in my head: smooth moulded Tupperware lids, the polished blue bonnet of our car, Neil Young's Heart of Gold, the plink plink plink of a tin table tapped lightly by rain one April day in Dorset.

You woke up and swore at me. I was pleased. I repented. I denied

I'd done it. But felt smug all the same, knowing I could still exercise control over you as you slept, pinching you into consciousness.

Where are you now in your dense sleep? Are you dreaming of me?

My sleep scrapbook comes to me in Technicolor before dawn; its pages spin and soar like a Busby Berkeley newsflash. My mother told me I'd only slept well for the first nine months after I was born. After that: awake all night. I think I taught myself how not to sleep in those months, as if I was gestating another baby, really I was growing my insomniac self. When I learnt to walk I learnt to sleepwalk too. My fatigue followed me around our house like a security blanket. As I got older, my nocturnal actions became more accomplished: teaspoons smeared in toothpaste dropped into the toilet bowl; porcelain ornaments hidden in the freezer; tender rosebuds picked carefully from their stems and arranged in a semicircle in front of the television; inch squares cut from the hems of clothes hanging in a wardrobe, then secreted in my size two school shoes. The night walks ceased when I was nine, when my father fell asleep forever. Was I afraid of bumping into him somewhere?

When the sleepwalking stopped, the Dream began. Always the same. A precise sequence that shocked me into wakefulness. Me. Small, waiting outside a door. Knowing what's going to happen. Set on a dream track that can't be diverted. Sick inside rising to my pigtails.

The door opens. A bright white empty room.

Featureless. Pristine. Perfect.

A huge sash window faces the doorway, letting in so much light the room sings with it: solid and humming, ushering me in.

Are they in the room already?

No. They are made suddenly from its glare.

Two men, two middle-aged men, clothed in dark suits. I'm terrified. I don't move. They glide towards me. I recognise their step, their stealth, their advancing speed. I wait.

Each plants a custodial hand on my shoulder; not restraining as such, for how could they check me when I was offering no resistance? Guiding me over to the sash window, one of them slides it open silently.

And there's something I'm feeling: something like a desire to please them.

I'm only nine in dream time. I'm four stone. I'm as light as a kitten. They toss me out the window.

As I fall, I see very little but I feel a lot. Air vents hold me firm, as the men's hands on my shoulders.

Every time, except the last, I wake up from the Dream in mid-air.

The last time: I was sixteen in reality, but still in the dream body of my nine-year-old self. I hit the ground. No pain, just relief, accompanied by a readjustment of the pavement around me. Content, I lie there sniffing it.

What does it smell of?

Petrichor: sunny rain.

The colour, well yes, the colour of the paving slabs reminds me of the elephant I saw in London Zoo the previous summer: a vast body of grey skin stretching out in front of me.

I cherish these secret steps my brain makes when it thinks I'm beginning to fall asleep, the confidential connections. If these sleep shortcuts are showing me my buried self, then maybe they're worth staying awake for. My generative dream tissue, it fuses, it fizzes, it endures: it makes sense.

Do you remember when we went to Dunwich four years ago? You told me the whole town had been swept into the sea by a storm in the thirteenth century, and that at certain tides, a careful listener can hear the church bells ringing. We walked along the coast, towards Sizewell power station.

I remember that day so well: one of the best we've had together in my reckoning.

Later, on the too soft B&B bed, sunken into its drooping mattress, I strained beside you to hear the bells' watery rings over your soft snoring. Anxiously, my mind began to burrow for alleviation. Confounded, until at last I recalled the polished surface of Sizewell's dome: a giant white ceramic egg near the beach. Its blankness soothed me, and as my feet struggled free of the heavy quilt, I imagined myself floating inside it.

Did I sleep right through, uninterrupted until the morning?

You know, I think I did.

# The
# Mech

anical
Copula

It is late and you're still up.[I]
May I?[II]
These eyes whose beauty all this world transcends
These arms, these hands, these slender feet
This face hath isolated me from mine own race
And hath made of me a stranger amongst my friends.
This wavy hair of pure and shining gold
This smile that ever turns my glum to mirth
Have made for me, a paradise on earth.[III]
I hope you will forgive the liberties I am taking with you madam, but I am very anxious to see you naked as Eve.[IV]
You don't protest?[V]
What a genius of an inventor your father must have been. Quite mad of course, but a poet to have made you so beautiful.[VI]
Did you lie with him, incestuously?[VII]
You tease me with your secret silence.[VIII]
Will you lie with me?[IX]
Will you abandon your delicate mechanisms to my desire?[X]
Yes. You will. Yes.[XI]
Don't spurn me.[XII]
What is your name? Rosalba? No, not Rosalba.[XIII]
No. I shall call you Love. Love. That is your name, isn't it?[XIV]
I've been looking for you all my... Always and... Oh! My little girl. My love, my love, oh, oh, oh my love, oh...[XV]
Yes.[XVI]
I love you. I love you. I love you. I love you. I love you. I love you. I love you. Love. Love. Love. Love. Love.[XVII]

[I] 1770. He: Giacomo Casanova, an infamous Italian libertine. Me: Rosalba, a finely wrought mechanical doll.
[II] Together: *Larvatus Prodeo.*

III When he addresses me, I want to answer, to express my delicate mechanisms, my fragile materials, my wooden thoughts. But my father made me without a voice, and so perhaps in vain, I try to show him. I try.

IV My skin is hard, yet gives to his touch. I have a solid core that holds me upright, but inside, I am soft for him.

V He forces his love upon me. So great his ardour, I am overwhelmed.

VI There were many before me but none so complete, so lifelike, so expressive. My sisters combined to form me. I am their daughter.

VII I have not always been so finely attired as I am now. Before I was brought here, I wore no clothes and felt no shame. That, I learnt.

VIII I creak. I click. I whirr. I sigh. Does he hear me?

IX I have been told there is another somewhat like me. Not like me. Like me. One which talks. One with no face, no lips, no tongue, but still a voice. It talks of love. What is that to me? I am Love.

X This other, this box with words, is filled with air. It is pushed and pulled and listened to.

XI I am pushed and pulled and listened to.

XII My dearest! My one and only Casanova! How might I show my love for you? Answer your passionate pleas?

XIII I give myself to you entirely. I tell you from my very fabric that you alone possess me. Hear me. I am Love. I will not be known by any other name, save that which you grant me.

XIV I creak. I click. I whirr. I sigh. My voice. He hears.

XV Under his force, my delicate mechanisms vibrate and spin and flutter and stutter and grip.

XVI He is inside me.

XVII I love you. I love you. I love you. I love you. I love you. I love you. I love you. Love. Love. Love. Love. Love.

# Bu
# Ki
# Drinkin

There is a true place beyond hangover (the area between riser and tread) where you are so parched and paranoid, you can't clock your own reflection in the bathroom mirror.

Unco indeed how he'd started out in fine fettle, but the stymied walk from the first to the second pub had been an odyssey of temper change.

There must be some way to moderate this feeling of lack, or perhaps excess (after the fact of course). If there is, he certainly doesn't know it. Now he would gladly eat out his own eyes to save his poor, poor head.

The curettage of solid, heavy drinking set him within a rumble of distant awe. Booze was amazing. It had even managed to transmogrify time last night in Burger King.

He ordered the special Tex-Mex quarter pounder with large fries, no doubt in a bar-room drawl *plus vin ordinare* than Texan. This burger tasted more burger than any he'd ever had before; the jalapeños weren't at all hot, rather chemical, as if laundered.

How long had he sat eating alone at the sticky table?

He knew he was supposed to be at the second pub at eight, but when he finally arrived, they told him it was well past ten already.

He will never ever and tomorrow drink again.

# Th
# Hea

Grace Pask was just a child herself when she gave birth to Ruby on a Sunday morning in March. The other new mothers on the maternity ward didn't talk to Grace. Even if they'd tried, they wouldn't have had much in common anyway, for Grace had just turned thirteen. The birth, considering her tender age and the baby's enormous weight of 12lb 10oz, was amazingly easy. Two and a half hours labour, no tearing or stitches, and discharged the following day; this combined with the fact that Grace hadn't shown any signs of being pregnant, made it seem as if the baby had simply appeared and not been born at all.

Grace was relieved to get back home to her mum, and her own room. The baby slept on the bed beside her for the first few nights, in a soft nest made from blankets. The whole thing had been such a rush, there'd been no time to buy a cot. Mrs Pask ordered one over the phone, there was just about enough room for it to slide in by the side of Grace's bed.

Right from the very beginning, baby Ruby slept the whole night through: a full nine-hour stretch. Well, not quite from the very beginning. Ruby hadn't slept in the hospital at all. She screeched so loud she'd disturbed all the other babies, until they joined her in an unbearable chorus of screaming: the maternity nurses were relieved when Ruby was taken home.

As soon as the infant was tucked up in Grace's room, she calmed down. Over the next few days, she settled into a solid routine; every three hours the baby woke, fed, then burped, dirtied her nappy, and lay patiently whilst Grace changed it. But mostly, Ruby slept.

The bus to Manchester trundled by Grace's window twice a day. She liked watching it pass. In return, the regular passengers liked tracking Grace's vigil, they felt pity when they saw her pale, slender face framed by a childish bob looking out. All of them, being local, knew about Grace's trouble, it was the talk of the village.

Most thought Grace wanted to leap out through her window, grip onto the top of the bus, and make a break for it to the big smoke. Some of them wondered when she'd go back to school, and if she'd ever be able to be a normal teenage girl. What they really wanted to know, however, was who had taken advantage of this young slip of a thing? What sort of brute had had his way with Grace, leaving her to deal with the consequences?

The passengers were wrong about one thing at least: Grace had no desire to escape.

"Mrs Pask, I've never seen anything like it. Ruby is such a bonnie baby," Nurse Kirby handed the infant back to Grace's mum. "She hasn't lost a drop of her birth weight, that's very unusual, most of them go down at least a few ounces."

"Oh, I'm so relieved Nurse Kirby. I was a bit worried, you know, after the birth and all, Ruby's just so big," Mrs Pask cuddled the baby into her body. "And just look at the size of my Grace, I don't know how she did it."

The midwife noted down Ruby's weight, together with any other observations she thought were important, in a thick red notebook she carried with her on home visits. She copied this information to the official files when she got back to the surgery, a system that had worked well for her for the last eighteen years.

Nurse Kirby sat down beside Grace, "Ruby's like a proper lady isn't she? Just look how strong she is, holding her head up all by herself... You're doing very well, love. You know, I've seen mums twice your age who can't cope at all. Well, your two weeks are up now for home visits from me, you'll have to bring the baby to the Health Centre from now on."

Grace liked Nurse Kirby well enough, but she was glad that from now on she wouldn't have to see the midwife every day.

Not only was Ruby the heaviest baby the midwife had in her care, she also had the most hair: full, soft brown curls set like a halo around her chubby face, and thick dark lashes that made her eyes look almost too expressive for a baby. It struck the nurse: Ruby really is like a tiny woman. She's come out almost fully formed.

Oh, and there was another thing, Ruby had been born with two teeth. Biggish ones on either side of the back of her mouth, nestled deep into the gums. This had alarmed Nurse Kirby at first, who'd never actually seen a newborn with teeth, she didn't comment on it to Grace or her mother, as she didn't want to upset them. They'd been through enough already.

One evening, after surgery had finished at the Health Centre for the day, Nurse Kirby sat at the office computer. She'd decided to search for other babies who'd been born with teeth and discovered sixteen individual cases in Croatia, Ireland, Spain and Italy—but all of those infants had incisor teeth. The only baby she could find like Ruby had been born in Brasilia. In 1989, an uncommonly large baby girl was delivered with four molars, when she was eleven weeks old, one of the teeth came out, lodged in her throat and choked her. Must keep an eye on baby Ruby, Nurse Kirby thought to herself, and shut down the computer.

Twice a week, Grace's mum ventured out to the village to do shopping and other errands. Whoever she met enquired after her daughter and of course the baby. Mrs Pask's answers were always polite and perfunctory, yet too sparse in detail to be of any real long-term interest. The villagers assumed her reticence was to do with shame. Grace's mother must be ashamed of having a thirteen-year-old daughter who herself has a baby girl. If they were in Mrs Pask's shoes, they would be.

Perfectly understandable.

They found it so frustrating though: who was the baby's father?

Surely it couldn't be one of the youngsters in the village—you'd be able to spot that type of guilt a mile off. Grace must've got pregnant in Manchester. And as for the baby's size, well! What with Grace being so petite, the father must be a monster, yes a monster in all senses! Maybe he'd got her drunk, talked her into, or forced her to have sex with him. Probably only the once. Unlucky. Grace Pask was one very unlucky girl.

But could anyone in the village remember seeing Grace ever getting the bus to Manchester? Could they remember seeing her going anywhere, other than to school and back? Could Kay in the Post Office, who pinned up the bus timetable beside her counter, recall Grace so much as looking at it, let alone buying a ticket? No. No, Kay would have to admit she couldn't remember anything like that at all. She thought long and hard about it, talked about it with other villagers, trying to work out exactly how Grace Pask had got pregnant. She hadn't even looked like she was expecting. Such a little lass, such a big baby. The whole thing was very confusing!

"Couldn't be any of the boys round here. Some other way," Kay confided in her customers, "must've been some other way. Grace's mother, she's always been a funny one, couldn't even hold on to that husband of hers. She might have a fancy man, and he's had his way with the girl too."

But when Kay discussed this with Mrs Pask's next-door neighbour, Gloria, whose intimate knowledge of local comings and goings was forensic, Gloria replied, "Sure as hell she's had no one in there, Kay, I would've noticed. Unless it was in the middle of the night, even then I'd have heard the front door. You know I don't get a wink with my Pete's snoring... "

"And Gloria," she steered the conversation back to the subject of Grace and Ruby, "have you seen Grace out much? With the baby at all?"

"No Kay, no I haven't. What do you think I do, sit here all day nosing out of my window?"

"But Gloria, " Kay persisted, "do you hear Ruby crying? These terraces, not being funny love, but you must hear the baby crying. They all do at that age, poor mites. Bit of colic. Don't like having their nappies changed, do they? It's their way of talking, isn't it?"

"Now you mention it Kay, I don't think I have done. Glad I am too. I don't think I could put up with all that racket again, now my two have gone... "

Grace watched as Kay left the house next door.

The Manchester coach was late. Normally it drove past Grace's window on its way back into the village at twenty past two, fifteen minutes before the baby woke up for her feed. Grace knew without looking Ruby was awake already: She could feel her baby's presence filling the room, and hear gentle rustling sounds coming from the cot, the tick-tock of Ruby's breathing gaining speed.

Grace lifted Ruby and then breastfed her whilst looking out of the window as the bus drove past. The baby sucked silently, as she always did for half an hour, after which she'd be winded and put back into her cot, before the cycle started again. And what did Grace do while Ruby slept? She checked her every now and then, especially at the beginning when she wasn't so used to Ruby being there, but mostly Grace looked out of the window, and thought.

They'd be expecting her to go back to school soon, after the first three months they made you, that's what Grace's mum had told her.

The school had been sending Grace homework, which she completed easily. Her mum brought the finished work back to the school office every Thursday and exchanged it for the new lot; Mrs Pask never checked her daughter's work, she trusted Grace to get on with it, and assumed the teachers must be happy with it too. There were no letters waiting with the secretary, no handwritten notes on the brown envelope the schoolwork came in, and no home visits from the teachers.

Even though she completed each bit of homework diligently, secretly Grace thought it was all a waste of time. She was thirteen now, only two years younger than her mum was when she'd left school to work at Woolworths, and exactly the same age as her granny had been scrubbing the doorsteps of big houses in Manchester six days a week.

Well, now Grace had a job. She had Ruby to look after.

Grace reckoned she'd learnt just about everything she needed to know. School had never been for her anyway, simple as that. The girls in her class whispered together, tied their ponytails up in the same style, gossiped about the teachers, and talked about the boys they fancied. Grace wasn't interested in all that. She was content sitting at her bedroom window, thinking how silly everyone outside looked rushing about the village.

Yes, they'd be expecting Grace to go back to school anytime now, and she really didn't want to.

Mrs Pask had accepted her daughter's predicament as best she could. She didn't quiz Grace on how she'd got pregnant, even though it did puzzle her. Grace went to a convent school for girls, she didn't go running around in a gang like most other youngsters in the village did, and at the weekends, even before Ruby was born, Grace preferred to stay in, helping about the house.

That's why everything that'd happened over the last months troubled Mrs Pask so much. She thought Grace might be feeling embarrassed or depressed, maybe a combination of the two. It would be entirely understandable if she was worried what the villagers thought about her: When Ruby is seven, Grace will only be twenty, she'll look like Ruby's sister, not her mother. She's worried what they're saying, that's why she wants to stay indoors all the time. Best not to push her, my Grace'll tell me when she's good and ready. It'll all sort itself out when she gets back to school.

What Mrs Pask didn't know was that Grace didn't care what the villagers thought about her. She was happy, very happy with things just as they were.

Ruby had been such a good feeder that Mrs Pask thought it was time to try her on the bottle. If Grace didn't have to be at home to breastfeed the baby all the time, then she could start going to school all the sooner.

The next time Grace's mum was in the village, she went to the chemist and bought a two-pack of baby bottles, three tubs of SMA formula and some Milton Sterilising Fluid. The chunky blue Milton bottle reminded Mrs Pask of when Grace had herself been born: when she was still married to John.

Every now and then, John used to take a notion to help her out: washing the baby bottles, pushing Grace about in the pram, things like that. He never changed a nappy though, or fed Grace, or got up in the middle of the night to put her dummy back in. No, not John, he'd had never done anything that looked like woman's work. He wasn't much use at helping anyway. To be honest, John Pask wasn't much use at anything. After he'd left them, Grace's mum didn't miss him at all. Not after the first couple of weeks at any rate.

As she walked back from the chemist, Mrs Pask asked herself if Grace could remember her father at all? Grace once said she had a vague memory of her daddy helping open Christmas presents. Grace's mum thought that was very unlikely, Grace had only been three when John left. In fact, Grace's mum knew it'd never happened. John was never out of bed that early on Christmas morning, he was always too hungover, having been out with mates on his annual Christmas Eve bender, with the excuse of going to Midnight Mass.

Grace's mum had accepted John had been brought up with certain beliefs: That's why he'd been so insistent on getting Grace baptised. Even the name—Grace—straight out of a hymn book. She hadn't minded about all that too much really; she'd even kept John's surname after they'd got divorced, along with the 'Mrs', so that Grace wouldn't get confused.

The woman did wonder though if she'd done the wrong thing in sending Grace to convent primary and secondary school. She'd had little choice, the schools were the only ones near the village. Grace didn't seem to mind, she never even mentioned school, let alone complained about it. But had the convent made Grace, well, a bit innocent, a bit silly about things to do with boys? If Grace'd been around boys more, she might have got more used to them, and then her curiosity wouldn't have got the better of her... Resolving there was no point in going over and over it, Grace's mum made a start on sterilising the bottles as soon as she got back home.

Grace did as her mother told her, she always had done, and to be fair it had usually worked out all right for both of them. Their terraced house was too small for arguments anyway. When the baby woke to be fed, Grace started her on breastfeeding, and then switched to the bottle.

But baby Ruby was having none of it. She didn't wrestle, or bawl, or fret. She just didn't eat.

Grace's mum told her, "Ruby's always been a great eater. Don't give in to her. When she's hungry, she'll take it from the bottle. She'll get used to it."

But Ruby didn't get used to it. What was worse, for the first time since she'd been born, she started to lose weight. Lots of weight. So much weight both Grace and her mum got very worried, very quickly, and brought Ruby to Nurse Kirby at the Health Centre.

The midwife was shocked when she saw the state the baby was in. After weighing and measuring Ruby, she told them, "Go back to breastfeeding immediately! Put away those bottles love, baby Ruby's just not ready yet. Dear, dear, any more big weight loss like this and we'll have to take her to the hospital."

The midwife moved them to the waiting room. She came back ten minutes later with a certificate signed by the doctor. It excused Grace from school for another three months, she gave it to the girl, "You'll have to stay at home looking after Ruby for a while longer, okay love?" Grace nodded.

Okay? Grace was delighted.

After just one week of breastfeeding, Ruby had plumped up considerably. Perfectly proportioned, long and sturdy, six-month-old Ruby looked more like a one-year-old.

Nurse Kirby started calling to Grace and Mrs Pask's again, every other day for two weeks, just to check the baby's weight, breathing, and teeth, making detailed notes in her book. The midwife was perfectly satisfied with Ruby's progress. The baby ate, the baby slept, the baby was growing like no other she'd seen, the baby obviously needed her mother.

Grace was getting homework sent from school, she was calm, happy, and healthy. Of course Grace was just a skinny thing, but then hadn't she always been? Hadn't Nurse Kirby delivered

Grace herself? Barely 6 lb. And whilst as a rule the midwife did not approve of children giving birth to children, she reminded herself: If Mrs Pask can accept Grace's baby with the brave face she's shown so far, well then so can I. Maybe something good'll come of all this after all.

Passengers on the Manchester bus, nearly all commuters, a few shoppers, had grown to look forward to seeing Grace's sallow face staring out at them. One or two even waved at her as they passed. In the main, the sight of the girl positioned at her window, sometimes with baby, sometimes not, made their journey that bit more bearable. More bearable, because they knew they were on their way to somewhere bigger, better, freer, and Grace, well little Grace Pask was stuck behind the window.

Grace never waved back. She didn't think the passengers' waving was intrusive exactly, she just couldn't see the point of it.

Grace had spent nine calm and happy months in her bedroom, soothed by the sounds of her mum moving around downstairs. Baby Ruby had grown so much, she was wearing clothes big enough to fit an eighteen-month-old, soon she'd need a new cot. All in all, things were working out well now for Grace, just as long as she didn't have to go back to school. She was learning more than she ever had done and it was such a relief not being filled with rules and prayers and gossip.

On a Thursday morning in December, Grace was woken early by a series of gripping pains low down in her body. She sat up in her bed, and rubbed her tummy. Ruby would be asleep until six. These dark mornings, Grace stayed in bed with the baby until her nine o'clock feed, when her mum would bring her some breakfast.

The pain again. This time worse, on and off for more than an hour. Grace felt it getting stronger and stronger, more regular too. She couldn't think of what else to do other than wake up her mum.

At 9.40am, Grace Pask was back in the labour ward. Her little body had made another baby girl.

'archetypes have no place here', first published as 'Their Nocturnal Poioumenon: Notes on *City of Women*', in *Jaki Irvine: City of Women* (Dublin: The LAB, 2010).

'Death Park', first published as 'Fieldnotes from the Urban Pastoral', in *Beyond Utopia* (Berlin: Errant Bodies Press, 2010).

'How You Lost the Stars', commissioned by Kadist Art Foundation (Paris: kadist.org, 2009).

'Sixteen Element Course on Mechanical Inelasticity', first published in *Volatile Dispersal: Festival of Art Writing Primer* (London: Book Works, 2009).

'The Mechanical Copula', first published in *Hey Hey Glossolalia* (New York: Creative Time, 2008).

'Spume', commissioned for *Nought to Sixty* (London: The Institute of Contemporary Art, 2008).

'Window Strikes', first published in *Copy Work* (Vancouver: Contemporary Art Gallery, 2007).

'1982, DOOM KNOTS', commissioned by Arcade Project (London: arcade-project.com, 2006).

Maria Fusco
*The Mechanical Copula*
Publisher: Sternberg Press

© 2010 Maria Fusco, Sternberg Press
All rights reserved, including the right of reproduction in whole or in part in any form.

Copyeditor: Matthew Evans
Design: Miriam Rech, Markus Weisbeck, Surface, Berlin/Frankfurt am Main

The author would like to thank Paula Fusco, Craig Martin, and all at Sternberg Press.

Printing and binding: Brandenburgische Universitätsdruckerei Potsdam
Typeface: Sabon, Jeanne Moderno
ISBN 978-1-934105-19-1

Sternberg Press
Caroline Schneider
Karl-Marx-Allee 78, D-10243 Berlin
1182 Broadway #1602, New York, NY 10001
www.sternberg-press.com